T2.FM.I-474

D0579430

By Lisa Westberg Peters

Illustrated by Barbara McGregor

Arcade Publishing / New York

To my mother — L.W.P.
To Mary and Ed — B.M.

First Edition

ISBN 1-55970-167-6
Library of Congress Catalog Card Number 91-58924
Library of Congress Cataloging-in-Publication information is available.

Published by Arcade Publishing, Inc., New York
Distributed by Little, Brown and Company
1 3 5 7 9 10 8 6 4 2
SC

Designed by Marc Cheshire

Printed in Hong Kong

Purple Delicious Blackberry Jam

Look, Grandma, berries! Freddy and Muff hold out a handful. Mmmm . . . juicy and sweet. They leave seeds in our teeth. Can we make jam, Grandma, blackberry jam?

Grandma snorts, Ha! Never do that sort of thing anymore. Too much work.

Freddy pleads, Oh please, Grandma, please?

Well . . . maybe just once. Where's my cookbook? Pots rattle; dust flies. Grandma runs a finger down the page. Here's an old recipe. All we need is the berries.

Grab a pail, kids. Let's go.

Grandma — ouch! — reaches into the thorniest bushes for the juiciest berries. Muff picks the little berries the birds don't want. Freddy scoops up the dropped ones.

Grandma pays the mosquitoes no mind. Muff squashes them flat. Freddy wears a bucket hat to hide from them.

At last, Grandma brings home a pail heaped with berries. Muff's pail has ten — whoops! — nine. And Freddy's pail is empty, but his tummy is full.

What do we do now? What does it say? Wash them and take out the red ones. Tumble and roll, into the strainer the blackberries go. No more eating, Freddy.

But look, there are sticks and leaves and little worms, too. Muff lines the worms up on the floor for a parade. Freddy giggles.

What's next? Mash and smash the berries? Little blops of juice squirt everywhere.

Enough! says Grandma. I need a wooden spoon.

Freddy grabs a bunch.

Sugar, says Grandma.

Muff finds it.

Bubble, burble, plop, ploop! The juice cooks up. Grandma reads through the steam and stirs. Who knows if it's ready? It must be.

She fills clean jars with frothy hot juice. Are we through? Muff asks. Nope, grumbles Grandma. Says here we have to seal the jars in boiling water. I'll set the timer.

We're hot enough! says Muff. Freddy swings open the fridge door for a cloud of cold air.

Ding!

Now we're through, right, Grandma? Grandma shakes her head.

Walls, floor, spoons, pans, Grandma's cheeks, and kids' hands — all purple.

Muff and Grandma scrub. Freddy sits in the corner and sags over, asleep.

Finally, by bedtime, the jars of jam are cool. Freddy and Muff slip slices of bread into the toaster. Grandma dips a knife into a jar. Uh-oh. Jam dribbles off her knife like soup.

What happened?

Grandma runs a purple finger down the page. Berries, yes. Sugar . . . no. We didn't use enough.

Grandma snorts, Ha! Never should have made jam. Too much work. Grandma slumps in her chair and sags over, asleep. Toast pops up and lands in a heap of dishes.

What can we do with all this soupy, drippy jam? Muff wonders.
Get a brush and paint Grandma's house?
Get a bottle and squirt it like glue?
Stir it with oatmeal and use it for bait?

Muff thinks and thumps her heels against the cupboard. Freddy thinks and taps a bowl with a spoon.

Thump. Tap.

Thump, thump. Tap, tap.

That's it! says Muff. We need bowls!

Freddy finds them.

And spoons! says Muff.

Freddy grabs a bunch.

Wake up, Grandma! Wake up!
Grandma drums her fingers on the table. What's this all about?

Muff dishes up. Freddy licks his lips.
Everyone digs in and smiles a purple delicious blackberry smile.

Purple
Delicious
Blackberry
~~Jam~~
Syrup